SCELIDOSAURUS

(ske-LI-doh-SAW-rus)

TYRANN

(tie-RAN-oh-SAW-

TRICERATOPS

(try-SER-a-tops)

STEGOSAURUS

(STEG-oh-SAW-rus)

APATOSAURUS

(a-PAT-oh-SAW-rus)

ANCHISAURUS

(AN-ki-SAW-rus)

SCELIDOSAURUS

(ske-LI-doh-SAW-rus)

TYRANNOSAURUS

(tie-RAN-oh-SAW-rus)

TRICERATOPS

(try-SER-a-tops)

STEGOSAURUS

(STEG-oh-SAW-rus)

APATOSAURUS

(a-PAT-oh-SAW-rus)

ANCHISAURUS

(AN-ki-SAW-rus)

This
Harry
book belongs to

....

Harry and the Dinosaurs and the Bucketful of Stories

Ian Whybrow and Adrian Reynolds

PUFFIN

PUFFIN BOOKS
Published by the Penguin Group: London, New York, Ireland, Australia, Canada, India, New Zealand and South Africa
Penguin Books Ltd, Registered Offices: 80 Strand, London WC2R 0RL, England

www.penguin.com

Harry and the Bucketful of Dinosaurs first published by David & Charles Children's Books 1999; published in Puffin Books 2003;
text copyright © Ian Whybrow 1999; illustrations copyright © Adrian Reynolds 1999
Harry and the Robots first published by David & Charles Children's Books 2000; published in Puffin Books 2003;
text copyright © Ian Whybrow 2000; illustrations copyright © Adrian Reynolds 2000
Harry and the Dinosaurs say "Raahh!" first published by Gullane Children's Books 2001; published in Puffin Books 2003;
text copyright © Ian Whybrow 2001; illustrations copyright © Adrian Reynolds 2001
Romp in the Swamp first published by Gullane Children's Books 2002; published in Puffin Books 2003;
text copyright © Ian Whybrow 2002; illustrations copyright © Adrian Reynolds 2002
Harry and the Snow King first published by Levinson Children's Books 1997; published in Puffin Books 2004;
text copyright © Ian Whybrow 1997; illustrations copyright © Adrian Reynolds 1997
This collection first published 2005
Published in this edition 2006
5 7 9 10 8 6

ISBN: 978–0–141–50009–6

Contents

Harry
and the
Bucketful
of
Dinosaurs

Nan thought the attic needed a clear out.
She let Harry help.
Harry found an old box
all grey with dust.

He lifted the lid . . .
DINOSAURS!

Harry took the
dinosaurs downstairs.

He unbent the
bent ones.

He fixed all the
broken ones.

He got up on a chair and washed them in the sink.
Nan came to see and say, "Just what do
you think you're up to?"

"Dinosaurs don't like boxes," Harry said.
"They want to be in a bucket."

Sam came in from watching TV.
She said it was stupid, fussing over so much junk.
"Dinosaurs *aren't* junk," Harry said.

The next day, Harry went to the library with Mum.
He took the dinosaurs in their bucket.

He found out all the names in a book
and told them to the dinosaurs.
He spoke softly to each one.
He whispered,
"You are my Scelidosaurus."
"You are my Stegosaurus."
"You are my Triceratops."

And there were enough names for all the Apatosauruses
and Anchisauruses and Tyrannosauruses.
The dinosaurs said, "Thank you, Harry."
They said it very quietly, but just
loud enough for Harry to hear.

After that, the dinosaurs went everywhere in Harry's bucket.

They went shopping.

They went to the garden centre.

They went to the beach.

When Harry had a bath, the dinosaurs had a bath.

When Harry went to bed,
the dinosaurs went to bed.

Sometimes they got left behind.
But they never got lost for long because
Harry knew all their names.

And he always called out their names,
just to make sure they were safe.

One day, Harry went on a train with Nan.
He was so excited, he forgot all
about the bucket.

Nan dried his eyes.
"Never mind," she said.
"I'll buy you a nice new video."

Harry watched the video with Sam.
It was nice, but not like the dinosaurs.

At bedtime, Harry said to Mum, "I like videos.
But I like my dinosaurs better
because you can fix them, you can bath them,
you can take them to bed.

And best of all, you can say their names."

Harry was still upset at breakfast next morning.
Sam said, "*Dusty old junk!*"
That was why Sam's book got milk on it.
Nan took Harry to his room to settle down.

Later, Nan took Harry back to the train station to
see the Lost Property Man.
The man said, "Dinosaurs? Yes we have found some dinosaurs.
But how do we know they are *your* dinosaurs?"

Harry said, "I will close
my eyes and call their names.
Then you will know."

And Harry closed his eyes and called the names.
He called,

"Come back

my Scelidosaurus!"

"Come back my Stegosaurus!"

"Come back my Triceratops!"

He called, 'come back', to the Apatosauruses
and the Anchisauruses
and the Tyrannosauruses
and all the lost old dinosaurs.
And when he opened his eyes . . .

. . . there they were – all of them standing on
the counter next to the bucket!
"All correct!" said the man.
"These are *definitely* your dinosaurs. Definitely!"

And the dinosaurs whispered to Harry.
They whispered very quietly, but
just loud enough for Harry to hear.
They said, "You are definitely *our* Harry, definitely!"

Going home from the station,
Harry held the bucket very tight.
Nan said to the neighbour, "Our Harry
likes those old dinosaurs."

"Definitely," whispered Harry.
"And my dinosaurs definitely like me!"
ENDOSAURUS

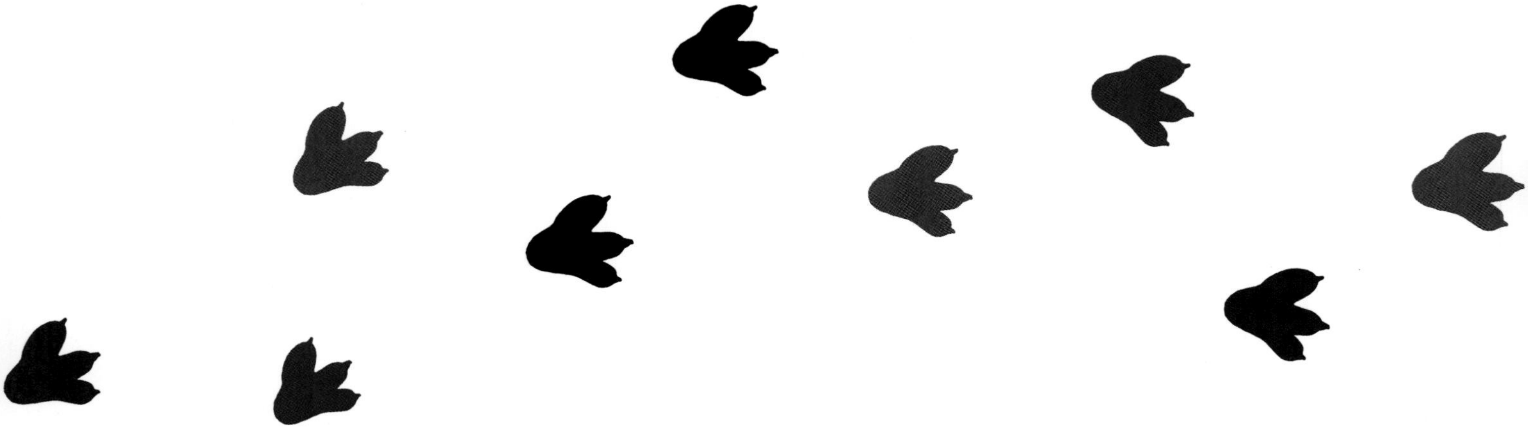

Harry
and the
Robots

It was a shock for Harry
when his robot fell over.
It was just doing a nice march
and suddenly its lights went out.

Harry heard Nan coughing in the yard,
so he ran out to show her.

Some of the robot's batteries had leaked onto its wires.
They put him in a parcel and sent him to the robot hospital.
"They'll know how to mend him," Nan said.

Harry wanted to make another robot to play with while he
waited for his marching robot to come back.
Nan said, "Good idea. We'll use my best scissors if you like."
They laid the things ready on the table.

But they never got started.
Mum made Nan go to bed,
her cough was so bad.

When Harry woke up the next morning, there was no Nan. The ambulance had come in the night. She had to go into hospital, Mum said, for her bad chest.

That day, Sam watched
TV a lot.

Harry started making a robot all by himself.
He wanted to use Nan's best scissors. Nan had said he could.
But Sam said, "No! Those are Nan's!"

That was why Harry threw his Stegosaurus at her.

Mum took him to settle down.
She said he could use Nan's best scissors if
Nan had said so, but only while she was
watching. He had to be very careful
though, because they were sharp.

Harry worked hard
all morning . . .

. . . until there was a new robot. A special one.
   Harry taught it marching. He taught it talking.
   But most of all he taught it blasting.
The robot said,
"Ha - Lo Har - Ree.
Have - you - got - a - cough?
BLAAAST!"

BLAAAST!

The hospital was big but they found Nan in there.

Mum said Sam and Harry had
to wait outside Nan's room.
They waved through the window
but Nan did not open her eyes.

Sam and Mum whispered with the doctor. So Harry
slipped into the room – just him and the special robot.

He put the special robot by Nan.
The robot said,
    "Ha - Lo - Nan.
        Have - you - got - a - cough?"
She opened one eye. It winked.
The robot said,
    "I - will - blast - your - cough.
        BLAAAST!"

BLAAAST!

That was when Mum ran in saying – "Harry! No!"
But the doctor said not to worry, it was fine.
A robot would be a nice helper for Nan.

That evening, Harry was very busy.

He joined . . .

he stuck . . .

he painted and . . .

Harry made five more
special robots to look
after Nan.

The robots guarded Nan.
They marched for her.
They blasted her cough.
And soon she was better.

Nan came home and unpacked her things.
"You're a good looker-afterer," she whispered.
"And my special robots," said Harry.
"Oh yes, them too," said Nan.
"I'd like to keep them by me, do you mind?"
Harry did not mind at all.

Nan went out into the yard to see how
the chickens were getting on.
They were just fine.

That afternoon a parcel arrived. It was the marching robot, back from the robot hospital. His light went on and he did a nice march – good as new.

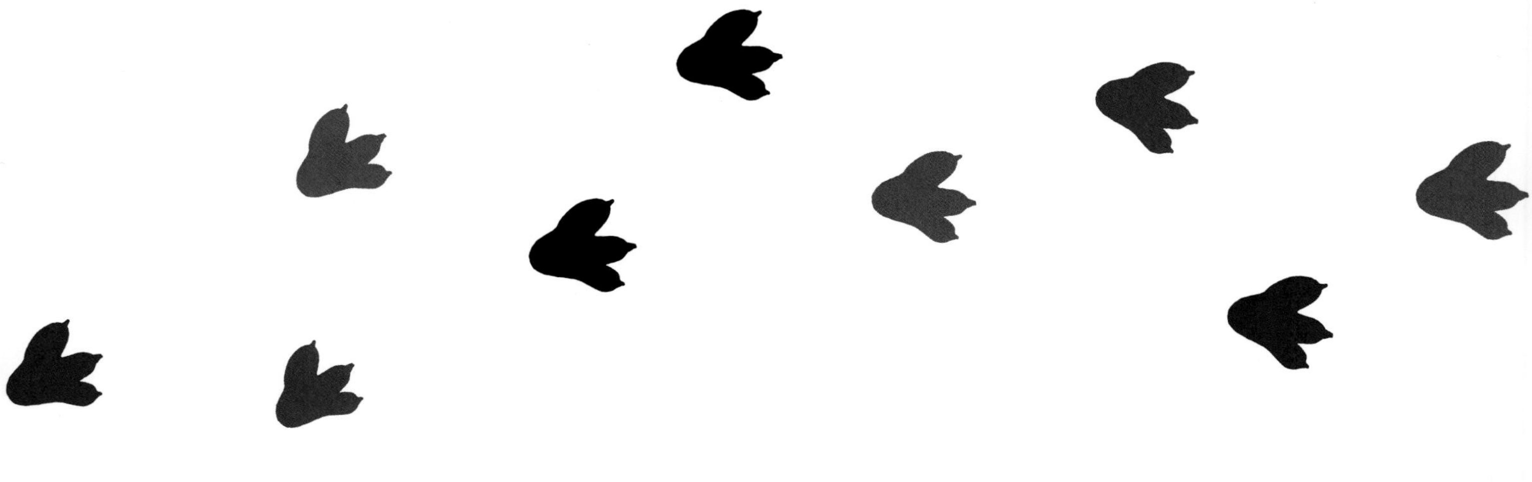

Harry and the Dinosaurs say "Raahh!"

Mum had her coat on,
but Harry was being slow.
They were going to see
Mr Drake, the dentist.

Harry was only a bit scared.
That was because of Sam
showing him her filling.

Harry wanted to take his dinosaurs,
but they were hiding all over the place.
He called all their names.

He said, "Get in the bucket, my Stegosaurus."
And out came Stegosaurus from under
the pillow.

He said, "Get in the bucket, my Triceratops."
And out came Triceratops from inside
the drawer.

And one by one, Apatosaurus and Scelidosaurus
and Anchisaurus all came out of their hiding
places and they jumped into the bucket.

All except for Tyrannosaurus. He didn't want
to go because he had a lot of teeth.
He thought Mr Drake might do drilling on them.

Harry said, "Don't worry, because when we get there,
I shall press a magic button on my bucket,
and that will make you grow big."

In the waiting room, the nurse said,
"Hello, Harry. Are you a good boy?"
Harry said, "I am, but my dinosaurs bite."

Then Mr Drake called,
    "Next please!"

The nurse took Harry into Mr Drake's room.
Harry wasn't sure about the big chair. He thought
maybe that was where Mr Drake did the drilling.
   "Come and have a ride in my chair," said Mr Drake.
"It goes up and down."
   Harry didn't want to ride.
   "Would one of your dinosaurs like a go?"
asked Mr Drake.

Harry put Tyrannosaurus on the chair.
He whispered to him not to worry,
then he pressed the magic button . . .
Tyrannosaurus grew VERY BIG!

"Open wide," said Mr Drake,
and then he turned around . . .

"RAAAAHH!" said Tyrannosaurus.
"Help!" cried Mr Drake, hiding behind the door. "Harry, what shall I do?"

Harry pressed the magic button.
Straight away, Tyrannosaurus
went back to being bucket-sized.

Harry felt safer now about getting
into the chair, so he climbed in with
his bucket. Then Harry and his dinosaurs
all had a ride together.
They opened their mouths wide for
Mr Drake and all went, 'RAAAAHH!'
Mr Drake said, "What a lot of teeth!
Will they bite me?"
Harry said, "They only bite drills."

"You are all good brushers," said Mr Drake,
"so no drills today, only a look
and a rinse."

All the dinosaurs liked riding and they liked rinsing.
  "Another bucket of mouthwash, Joan!"
called Mr Drake.

Going home, Mum let Harry choose a book
from the library for being so good.
  "Let's have a shark book!" said Harry.
  "RAAAAHH!" said the dinosaurs.
"Sharp teeth! We like sharks!"

ENDOSAURUS

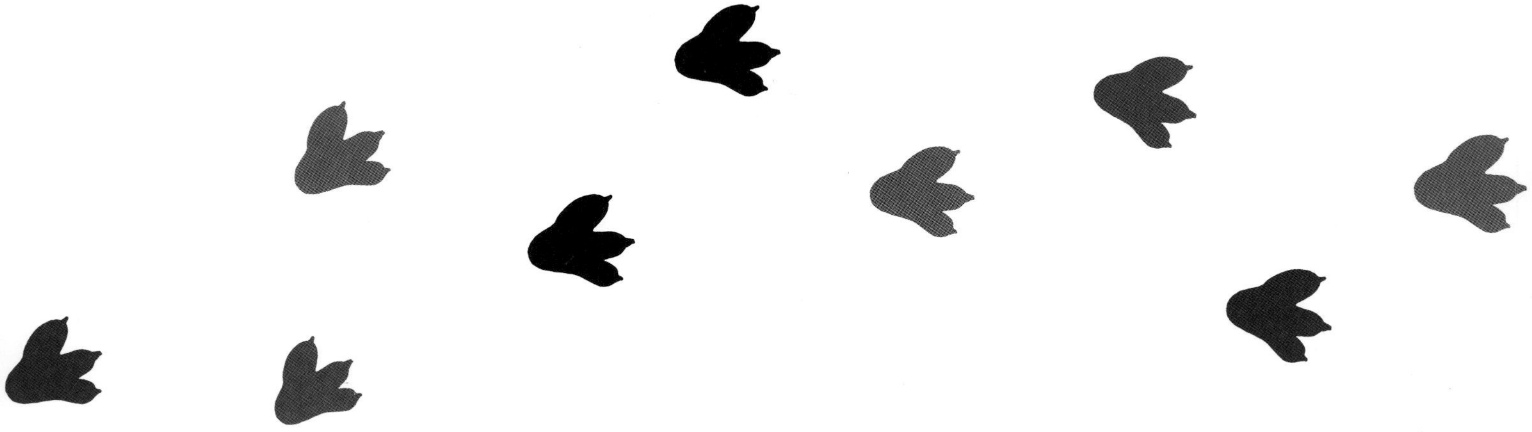

Romp
in the
Swamp

Mum and Nan were taking Sam to see her new school. That was why Harry and the dinosaurs had to go and play with some girl called Charlie.

Harry called their names but
the dinosaurs were hiding.

"Don't let Charlie play with us, Harry," said Apatosaurus.
"She might do bending on our legs," said Anchisaurus.
"She might chew our tails," said Triceratops.
"She won't understand about dinosaurs," said Scelidosaurus.

"Don't worry," said Harry. "You get in the bucket.
I won't let anyone else play with *my* dinosaurs."

"What took you so long, slowcoach?" said Sam.
"None of your business!" said Harry.
Good thing Nan sat between them.

Charlie and her mum came to the door to meet Harry.
Harry hid the dinosaurs behind his back.

"Goodbye!" called Mum. "Have a good time!"
Harry and the dinosaurs didn't think they would.

Charlie went inside and
sat on the sofa with her toys.

Harry sat at the other end of the sofa.
He guarded the dinosaurs and wouldn't speak.

Then Charlie went off
and found a big basket.
In went her dumper truck
and her tractor.

In went some cushions,
in went some boxes.

In went some pans
and some plants and
some string.

Harry and the dinosaurs
followed her into the garden.
 "What is she doing?"
whispered Harry.

"She's making a primeval forest!" said Anchisaurus.
"And a primordial swamp!" said Triceratops.
"That looks fun!" said Stegosaurus.

"Hisssssss"

went the hose like a great big snake.

"Look out!" Harry shouted.
"That snake might bite us!
Oh no, he's squeezing
Tyrannosaurus!
Quick! Save him!"

Harry and the dinosaurs joined in the noisy game.
Anchisaurus went crash with the tractor.
Scelidosaurus went bump with the dumper truck.
Apatosaurus and Triceratops made a strong
snake-lead out of string.
Stegosaurus grabbed the snake's tail.

"Help me with the snake cage!" shouted Charlie.
Whump went the snake cage and
captured the snake!

"Raaaah!"
said Tyrannosaurus.
"You can't catch me,
Mister Snaky!"

Then everyone did a noisy capture-dance.

"Hooray!" said Charlie. "What shall we do now?"
"Let's all have a feast!" said Harry.

"Would you like to play with
Charlie another day?" called Mum.
"Definitely!" said Harry.
"Definitely!" said the dinosaurs.

ENDOSAURUS

Harry
and the
Snow
King

When the snow came, you had to look for it.
But Harry had waited long enough.
He went out with his spoon and plate.

He put out his tongue and caught a flake.
It was just right.

There was some in the corner by the woodpile.
There was a good bit by the henhouse.

And if you were very careful
you could scoop it off the leaves.

It took all morning to find enough snow
to make the snow king.

Nan called, "What are you doing out there?"
"Nothing," he said. But he was looking
on the holly for red buttons.

Mum called, "Are you hungry?"
"Not yet," he said.
He was hungry, but he was making a crown.

Sam said, "Your soup is cold, stupid."
"Coming," he said, and brought the
snow king to show them.

They all bowed down to look.

Sam said not to bring him in,
it was too warm inside.

That was why Harry left
the snow king on the wall.

He ate his soup and told about the snow king.

Sam said big snowmen were better and he was stupid not to have waited.

That was why Harry threw his bread at Sam.

Nan took him to his room
to settle down.

Later, the snow king was not on the wall.

"You just give him back!" Harry said.
But Sam had been watching TV all the time.

The snow king was
nowhere in the yard.
He was not in the refrigerator.

"Somebody kidnapped him," said Harry.

He wanted to call the police
but Mum said better not to bother them.

Four o'clock, Mr Oakley passed
on his tractor. Harry said
about his snow king
being kidnapped.

Mr Oakley looked up at the sky.
He said not to give up hope.
He said maybe the snow king
went to order more snow.

Next morning there were
snowpeople all over the yard.

Ten at least. Wonderful!
And white everywhere, everywhere you looked!

Mr Oakley drove by on his way back from milking. "I found these earlier," he said. He opened his hand to show the red buttons and the crown.

"I hoped all night," said Harry.
"I never gave up. It was just like you said.
The snow king went to order some more snow,
but he left me these snowpeople."

"Hitch up your sledge," said Mr Oakley.
"This looks like good snow for getting towed
by a tractor. Shall we go now, or wait for Sam?"

"Sam's watching TV," said Harry.

"We'll come back for her later then,"
said Mr Oakley. "You get first go."

Harry and Sam had a lot of fun that day.
But, that first go was just the best.

Look out for all of Harry's adventures!

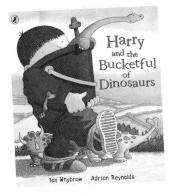

ISBN 0140569804

Harry and the Bucketful of Dinosaurs

Harry finds some old plastic dinosaurs and cleans them, finds out their names and takes them everywhere with him – until, one day, they get lost...Will he ever find them?

ISBN 0140569863

Harry and the Snow King

There's just enough snow for Harry to build a very small snow king. But then the snow king disappears – who's kidnapped him?

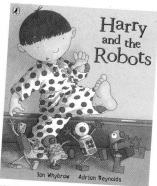

ISBN 0140569820

Harry and the Robots

Harry's robot is sent to the toy hospital to be fixed, so Harry and Nan decide to make a new one. When Nan has to go to hospital, Harry knows just how to help her get better!

ISBN 0140569812

Harry and the Dinosaurs say "Raahh!"

Harry's dinosaurs are acting strangely. They're hiding all over the house, refusing to come out...Could it be because today is the day of Harry's dentist appointment?

Harry and the Dinosaurs at the Museum

When Harry and the dinosaurs go to the museum, the dinosaurs want to get out of their bucket and meet their ancestors but don't want to get lost. Then Harry starts playing with them and before long he's lost! Will Mum and Nan know where to find him?

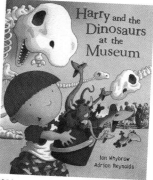

ISBN 0141380187

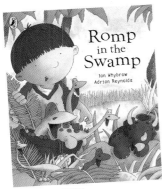

ISBN 0140569847

Romp in the Swamp

Harry has to play at Charlie's house and doesn't want to share his dinosaurs. But when Charlie builds a fantastic swamp, Harry and the dinosaurs can't help but join in the fun!

Harry and the Dinosaurs make a Christmas Wish

Harry and the dinosaurs would *love* to own a duckling. They wait till Christmas and make a special wish, but Santa leaves them something even more exciting…!

ISBN 0141380179 (hbk)
ISBN 0140569529 (pbk)

ISBN 0140569839

ISBN 0140569855

Harry and the Dinosaurs play Hide-and-Seek
Harry and the Dinosaurs have a Very Busy Day

Join in with Harry and his dinosaurs for some peep-through fold-out fun! These exciting books about shapes and colours make learning easy!

SCELIDOSAURUS
(ske-LI-doh-SAW-rus)

TYRANNOSAURUS
(tie-RAN-oh-SAW-rus)

TRICERATOPS
(try-SER-a-tops)

STEGOSAURUS
(STEG-oh-SAW-rus)

APATOSAURUS
(a-PAT-oh-SAW-rus)

ANCHISAURUS
(AN-ki-SAW-rus)